On Pins and Needles

A Christmas Tale

Enjoy! CR Young

by Carole R. Young

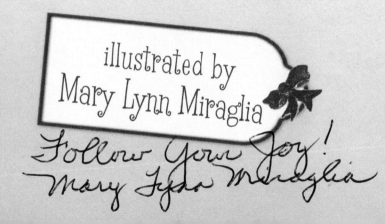

illustrated by
Mary Lynn Miraglia

Follow Your Joy!
Mary Lynn Miraglia

Published by:
CDM Publishing
Webster, NY

Text copyright © 2017 by Carole R. Young
Illustrations copyright © 2017 by Mary Lynn Miraglia

ISBN: 978-0-69293-776-1

Cover and interior layout by Gary A. Rosenberg
www.garyarosenberg.com

Other Books by Carole R. Young

The Runaway Egg

Nathan and the Note Nerd

for

MeMe

Sister and best friend

—C. Young

for

Dorothy

Mom, my forever cheerleader

—M. L. Miraglia

It was Christmas Eve, and all was in readiness at our house. Our two children, Becky & Bobby, had hung up their stockings and set out cocoa for Santa and carrots for his reindeer.

Now, they were snuggled in their beds trying very hard to go to sleep, so Santa would come.

1

Downstairs, in our living room, my husband Don
had made a fire in the fireplace. My mother and
I were enjoying its warmth and the lovely aroma
of our stately pine tree standing in the corner.

Sitting on the couch together, Mom said, "Carole,
do you recall the year our Christmas tree fell down?"

"Oh Mom," I chuckled. "How could I ever forget!"

It was another Christmas Eve long ago, when I was just 5 years old and my sister, MeMe, was 7. Our mother had just given us some really exciting news.

We WOULDN'T have to go out with our parents to deliver the Swedish breakfast rings our Mom made each holiday season for our neighbors.

Mom was known all over our small town for her delicious breakfast treat. Raised dough was braided and then shaped into a wreath and baked.

Once out of the oven, Mom would drizzle vanilla frosting on the top and finish off each wreath with chopped walnuts and bright red Maraschino cherries.

The recipe was part of our mother's Swedish heritage, and she remembers her parents delivering the same baked goods to their neighbors when she was a little girl.

5

When we were younger MeMe and I dreaded those yearly delivery trips. For some reason our neighbors were mostly older people, so there were few children to play with once we got to their homes. Each Christmas season Mom would remind us to be on our best behavior.

"When we get to the Stubbs' home take off your galoshes even though Mrs. Stubbs says you don't have to.

"Don't ask Mrs. Milillo to repeat something she has said that you don't understand. Italian is her first language, and sometimes she has a hard time expressing herself in English.

"Don't ask Miss Lee why she has blue hair. It's the style for older ladies to dye their gray hair with a blue rinse."

Once we arrived at our neighbors' homes, it was mostly grownups talking and we two girls sitting quietly on stiff horsehair sofas.

7

But this year was going to be different. We DIDN'T have to go!
We were old enough now to stay home. We lived in a double
house, and our Gramma GaGa and Great Aunt Key lived on
the other side. They would keep a protective eye on us.

The moment our parents closed the front door,
MeMe and I began to make plans.

"Let's play hide and seek," MeMe suggested.
Being the older sister she often had good ideas,
so I readily agreed.

"OK. I'll hide first. You go in the kitchen and
count backwards from 100 – SLOWLY!"

MeMe began "100 . . . 99 . . . 98 . . ."

9

Our old house was pretty big – 4 floors in all – so I had plenty of places to hide. The basement was too dark, I thought, and the attic too cold. That left two floors to choose from.

Upstairs might be a problem. Perhaps MeMe could hear me climbing the creaky stairs.

I decided downstairs was the best place to search out the perfect hiding place. Hmmm, behind the couch? I wondered.

Maybe, but I'd have to pull it away from the wall, and it was a very heavy couch. And, MeMe might notice it was not exactly in its usual up-against-the-wall place.

Behind our large floor-model radio?
I don't think so. Daddy would be
mad if he knew I'd hidden there.
Too many scary electrical things!

Then I spied the PERFECT place. I'd hide behind the Christmas tree. There were lots of packages under the tree ready to be opened the next morning.

I tip-toed carefully among the gifts, balancing on one foot as I wiggled my other foot between the prettily wrapped packages. All went well for my first couple of steps.

Then, suddenly, I lost my balance. All these years later I don't remember exactly what happened next, but both the tree and I went crashing down.

Glass Christmas ornaments shattered, the bright tree lights went dark, and I was lying among the green branches covered with pine needles and silver icicles.

13

I didn't run next door to tell GaGa and Key what had happened. I didn't call out to MeMe. Instead, as fast as my legs could carry me, I ran upstairs into my bedroom, yanked back the blankets and sprang into bed.

I pulled up the covers over my whole body, even my head. Perhaps, in my 5-year-old mind, I thought if I couldn't see what happened, maybe, just maybe, it hadn't happened at all.

I remember crying in great sobs, thinking I had ruined Christmas. And, of course, I worried about what Mommy and Daddy would say when they got home.

My next clear memory is my mother sitting next to me on the bed. She pulled me out from under the covers, placed me on her lap, and wrapped her arms around me. Gently, she wiped my drippy nose with her white linen handkerchief.

"Carole, can you tell me what happened to our Christmas tree?" she asked.

I blurted out between sobs, "I don't know Mommy. I wasn't anywhere near the tree when all of a sudden it just fell down."

Mom continued rubbing my back to calm me.

Finally, she said, "Daddy is downstairs. He thinks the tree is going to be OK. Why don't we go down and see if we can help."

17

I wasn't so sure the tree was OK. And I wasn't too excited to see Daddy either. He could be quite stern at times.

Mom took me by the hand and led me back downstairs. Daddy was running the vacuum cleaner over the broken glass and pine needles. He didn't look at me. He had his stern face on.

I stood behind the chair watching, being very quiet, something quite unusual for me. Once the tree was back up it looked almost as pretty as it had before I tipped it over. Daddy got the lights working again. Mom, MeMe and I replaced the scattered tinsel and the "still good" ornaments.

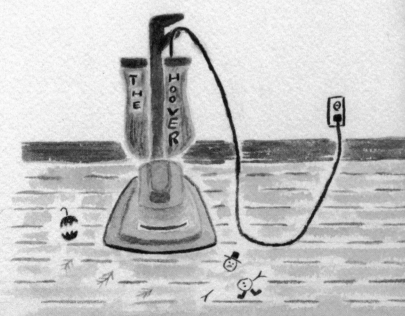

Then, perhaps because Mom sensed there was still some tension in the air, she sat down at our grand piano next to the tree and played Christmas carols.

I don't remember returning that night to the bedroom my sister and I shared. Maybe we fell asleep listening to the music and were carried up to bed by our parents.

I do remember the next morning. Santa had come! Daddy was smiling again! Both MeMe and I got new dolls which we promptly dressed in outfits beautifully handcrafted by GaGa and Key.

21

Daddy brought up from the basement an amazing
two-story doll house he had made. It was painted
white with green shutters. Two evergreen trees
stood proudly on either side of the red front door.

We were beyond thrilled! It was a spectacular gift –
one we didn't have a clue he was making. So, what
had started out as a pretty awful Christmas Eve
turned out to be an absolutely perfect Christmas Day.

"So, Mom, did I recall the day correctly?" I asked.

"Just about perfectly," she responded, "even the part about your Dad and I carrying you and MeMe upstairs that Christmas Eve."

Putting her hand over mine as we sat together on the couch these many years later, she said, "There's just one additional detail. All the while I was holding you on my lap in your bedroom, and you were crying, I was carefully picking pine needles out of your hair."

The End

Afterword

Two months after this story took place our little sister, Betsy, was born. I was so excited about rushing home from school to see our brand new baby sister (in those days children could not visit maternity wards) that I broke the glass cupboard door in which I had just placed, too hastily, our class reading books. My parents must have wondered what my next accident-prone "adventure" might be.

We three girls happily spent all our growing up years in that big double house in Auburn, NY, surrounded by our loving family and the neighbors mentioned in this book. MeMe and I shared the same back bedroom and the same double bed until she went off to college at age 18.

Our parents have been gone for some time now, but the lesson they taught me that Christmas Eve about forgiveness is one I will always remember.

MeMe passed away recently at age 78. Today, Betsy and I live just 10 minutes apart in Webster, N.Y.

Carole & MeMe, circa 1944

Acknowledgments

From the Author

Writing a book is never a solitary journey. I am very grateful to the following people who helped bring this book to life. When I began writing this story I could not reconcile whether I should place it in the past or present tense. Book club friend, Darlene Piersall, suggested I start it in the present tense, write the bulk of the story in the past tense, and then return to the present for the end of the book. It turned out to be the perfect solution.

Once the story was written, several friends read the draft, each one suggesting ideas that clarified details and enhanced the story. Thank you, Becky Young, Kathy Whitlock, and Betsy Reed. It was sister Betsy who, after reading an early draft, thought of the perfect title, "On Pins and Needles."

In a stroke of good luck I met, by chance, an artist at a Rochester Retired Teachers' meeting. Mary Lynn Miraglia graciously took on the considerable task of creating 19 vintage drawings to match the story line of this book. Her winsome and charming illustrations on these pages are the wonderful result. Mary Lynn's warm and upbeat personality made her an absolute delight to work with and a person I now feel blessed to call a friend.

Working with Gary Rosenberg at The Book Couple (gary@thebookcouple.com) was a very positive experience. Knowledgeable and detail oriented, he clearly outlined every phase of book production. The fact that Gary was also prompt, patient, and good humored were added bonuses.

Finally, I am particularly grateful to my husband, Donald, who is both an expert editor and typist, and always my most ardent literary supporter.

From the Illustrator

When I received Carole's call to consider illustrating "her" childhood Christmas story, I was excited and at the same time concerned about the challenge to create the visuals that would match her special childhood memories. I knew my time commitment in the year ahead would have a very new focus.

Thus I would like to give special thanks to my husband, John, for his patience, support, and critical eye throughout this process. I also thank my other family members, especially my daughters Jen and Meg, painting instructors and painting friends, especially my dear friend Carol Lennox, for their suggestions, tips, and their consistent encouragement. Thanks also to photographers Dan Abbas and Dan Hucko for their skills and friendship, and to little Emma and her grandmother Marilyn Jesserer for being willing and excellent models.

Participation in this creative journey with Carole Young was a wonderful challenge and a continuous reminder that it is never too late, and always right to pursue that which gives you joy.